My Family

People in My Family

By Sophie Geister-Jones

level 2 little blue readers

www.littlebluehousebooks.com

Little Blue House is distributed by North Star Editions:
sales@northstareditions.com | 888-417-0195

Produced for Little Blue House by Red Line Editorial.

Photographs ©: eli_asenova/iStockphoto, cover; monkeybusinessimages/iStockphoto, 4, 20, 24 (top right); kali9/iStockphoto, 7; PeopleImages/iStockphoto, 8–9; Dmitry Naumov/Shutterstock Images, 11; LuckyBusiness/iStockphoto, 12; davidf/iStockphoto, 15; gradyreese/iStockphoto, 16–17; bjones27/iStockphoto, 19; FluxFactory/iStockphoto, 22–23; Flamingo Images/Shutterstock Images, 24 (top left); Theeradech Sanin/Shutterstock Images, 24 (bottom left); MongPro/Shutterstock Images, 24 (bottom right)

Library of Congress Control Number: 2019908259

ISBN
978-1-64619-038-6 (hardcover)
978-1-64619-077-5 (paperback)
978-1-64619-116-1 (ebook pdf)
978-1-64619-155-0 (hosted ebook)

Printed in the United States of America
Mankato, MN
012020

About the Author

Sophie Geister-Jones likes reading, spending time with her family, and eating cheese. She lives in Minnesota.

Table of Contents

My Family

I am part of a family.
My family has
many people.

My mom takes me to the playground. She goes down the slide with me.

mom

My dad plays music
with me.
He plays his guitar.
I bang on pots and pans.

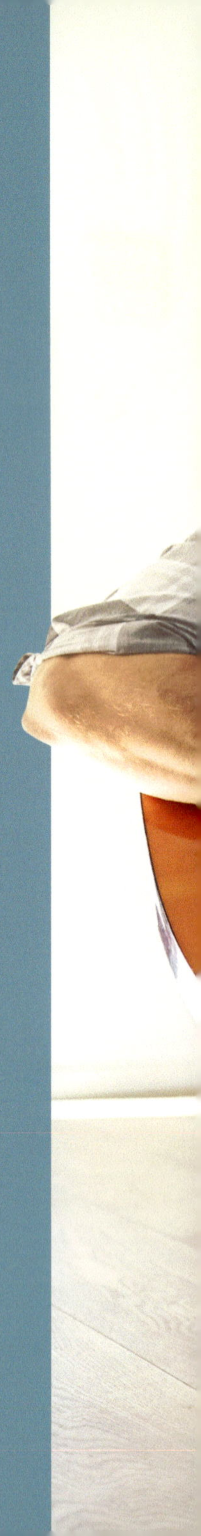

dad

I have a big brother, and I have a little sister.

We like to play together.

sister
brother

grandma
apron

Other Family Members

Sometimes I visit
my grandma.
We put on aprons and
make cookies.

My grandpa reads books with me.

He is very special to me.

grandpa

My dad has a sister.

She is my aunt.

I like dancing with her.

aunt

My mom has a brother.
He is my uncle.
I like going to the
playground with him.

uncle

pet

All Different

Families can be big.

Families can be small.

Some families have pets.

All families look different.

But they are all families.

Glossary

apron

pet

guitar

playground

Index